Dear Reader,

Suppose you had to win a football game against a team that was bigger than you. Their team practices a lot. They also have fancy uniforms.

Meanwhile, your team doesn't have any experience. You're not so big and you have no uniforms. Can you win?

That's what Molly and her Pee Wee Scout friends are asking themselves. *Blue Skies, French Fries* is all about an exciting big game. It's also about teamwork and confidence.

You'll discover how the Pee Wee Scouts raise money for a good cause. You'll also meet the twins, Molly's newest friends, and Sonny, the timid boy who can't seem to do anything right. As you read this book, try to guess what will happen next.

Sincerely,

Stephen Fraser

Stephen Fraser
Senior Editor
Weekly Reader Book Club

Weekly Reader Books Presents

Blue Skies, French Fries

JUDY DELTON

Illustrated by Alan Tiegreen

A YOUNG YEARLING BOOK

This book is a presentation of Newfield Publications, Inc.
Newfield Publications offers book clubs for children
from preschool through high school. For further
information write to: **Newfield Publications, Inc.,**
4343 Equity Drive, Columbus, Ohio 43228.

Published by arrangement with Dell Publishing,
a division of Bantam Doubleday Dell Publishing Group, Inc.
Newfield Publications is a trademark of Newfield Publications, Inc.
Weekly Reader is a federally registered trademark
of Weekly Reader Corporation.

Published by
Dell Publishing
a division of
Bantam Doubleday Dell Publishing Group, Inc.
666 Fifth Avenue
New York, New York 10103

ISBN: 0-440-40064-3

Printed in the United States of America

September 1988

10 9 8 7 6 5

W

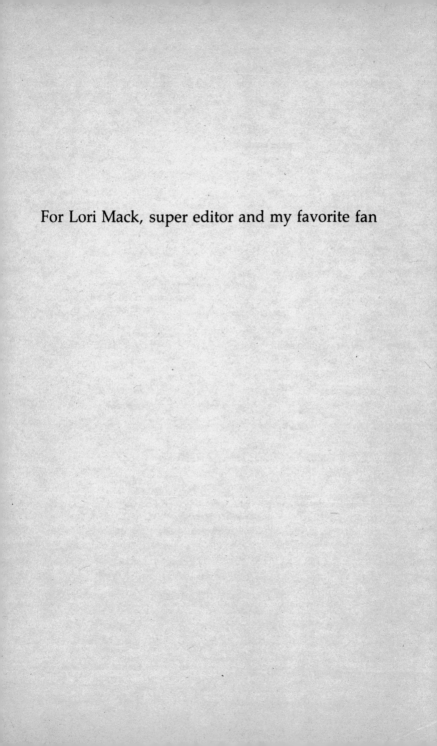

For Lori Mack, super editor and my favorite fan

Contents

Contents

CHAPTER 1

Second Grade

It was the last day in August. The last day of summer vacation.

"Rat's knees!" said Molly Duff. "School starts tomorrow."

"But the next day," said Mary Beth Kelly, "we have our Pee Wee Scout meeting."

That cheered Molly. She loved Pee Wee Scouts. But she didn't love school.

1

This year, when school opened, they would be in second grade.

Second grade sounded like a lot of work. Even homework. A new teacher and new books.

Many of the Pee Wees were seven years old already.

"We better play fast," said Mary Beth.

But Molly and Mary Beth didn't feel like playing.

"I have to get my stuff ready for school," said Molly.

"I've got a new *Star Wars* lunch box," said Mary Beth.

"I've got a folder to hold my papers," said Molly.

Molly had wanted a folder for a long time. Ever since kindergarten. Now she would have enough papers to use one.

In second grade you used lots of paper. Piles of paper!

2

"See you tomorrow," said Mary Beth, going down the street to her own house.

Molly waved.

The next morning Molly's mother had her clothes laid out for school. Her new plaid skirt. A new white blouse. Even a new hair ribbon.

Vacation was over.

The first day went fast. Even though Molly grumbled about it.

There were some new students in her room. And sharp new pencils and clean, shiny desks. Everything was new except the smell. Molly made a face.

That school smell was the same as in first grade.

The next day, Molly watched the clock move toward Pee Wee Scout time.

Three o'clock.

3

Then she could dash out the door with the other Scouts to Mrs. Peters's house. Mrs. Peters was their leader.

As soon as the little hand got to three, Molly jumped out of her seat. She ran out the door.

"Molly!" called Mrs. Harris. "The bell has not rung yet."

Rats, thought Molly. What was the matter with that bell? The clock said three o'clock.

"Now sit down and be patient, dear," said her new teacher. "In second grade we are grown up, aren't we?"

No, said Molly to herself. I am still six. I'm not grown up.

"Now we will all just sit here until we are grown up," said Mrs. Harris.

That could take forever, thought Molly. Eighteen years!

The bell rang. Mrs. Harris held up her

hand. It meant "stay." It was what Mrs. Peters said to Lucky when she wanted him to stay! Lucky was their troop mascot.

The whole class glared at Molly. This was her fault they were staying after school.

That they had to wait.

That some of them would be late for Scouts.

Everyone else in the school was leaving. Molly could hear them outside. Shouting and calling to each other. Getting on buses.

But the second grade sat still.

The big hand of the clock moved past twelve, on its way to one.

"Dummy!" whispered Rachel Myers to Molly. "It's all your fault."

Just when the Pee Wees could sit still no longer, Mrs. Harris said, "Class dismissed."

The Pee Wee Scouts walked quietly to the door. But when they got there, they ran!

All the way to Mrs. Peters's house!

CHAPTER 2

A Double Surprise

Mrs. Peters was waiting. The Scouts tumbled in her front door. They had on their Pee Wee Scout kerchiefs that said Troop 23.

Molly looked to see if Mrs. Peters was getting fat. She was supposed to get fat because she was going to have a baby.

Molly knew that.

8

Most of the Pee Wees knew that. Except maybe Sonny Betz. He was a mama's boy. He probably doesn't know where babies come from, thought Molly.

"Maybe Mrs. Peters will have her baby on Labor Day," whispered Lisa Ronning to Molly.

Molly had thought the same thing. Mrs. Peters did look fatter.

But not fat enough to have a whole baby.

"Naw," whispered Molly. "Labor Day is next week. She can't have her baby next week."

The Scouts held hands and said their Pee Wee Scout pledge. Then they told about the good deeds they had done that week. And about the people they had helped.

"I helped my dad clean the refrigerator," boasted Tracy Barnes.

"I took my baby sister for a long walk," said Lisa. "So my mom could take a nap."

"Helping others begins at home," said Mrs. Peters. "It's good to help your family."

Molly couldn't remember a single good deed she had done.

Pretty soon everyone had told a good deed but her.

"Molly?" said Mrs. Peters. "Would you like to share something you did to help?"

Molly thought fast.

She had tried to help an old lady cross the street. But the lady did not want any help. She had said, "I can do it myself."

Then Molly had gone to the store for her aunt, but she got the wrong brand of peanut butter. Her mother told her to take it back. That was not much help.

"I didn't do anything," Molly admitted.

Mrs. Peters thought a minute. "I know

10

something you did," she said. "You took
Lucky for a walk."

Lucky barked. Then he licked Molly's
face. Molly smiled. She had forgotten that.

The Scouts clapped for Molly.

Suddenly there was a knock on the
door. The Pee Wees wondered who it

could be. All of the Scouts were already there.

Mrs. Peters went to the door. "Come in," she said.

Two children and their mother walked in.

"Boys and girls, this is Mrs. Baker. Patty and Kenny are going to join our troop today," said Mrs. Peters.

New Scouts! They looked bashful. Molly knew how they felt. It was awful to be new.

"Patty and Kenny are twins," said Mrs. Peters. "They are new to our city and we will all try to make them feel welcome."

Twins! Molly didn't know any twins.

Mrs. Peters gave them Scout kerchiefs. Rachel ran up and helped them tie them around their necks.

Rats, why didn't I think of that? thought Molly.

The twins looked alike. They both had short brown hair. They had on matching shirts.

Mrs. Baker left, and Rachel showed the twins where to sit. Right beside her.

"Our new members are one of my surprises today," said Mrs. Peters. "My next surprise is our Pee Wee weenie roast next Saturday. I have talked to your moms and dads and they are all making something good to eat. We'll have a big bonfire and roast weenies and marshmallows and Indian corn," she said.

"What's Indian corn?" asked Rachel. "My dad doesn't like me to eat foreign food."

The Scouts snickered.

"It will be a surprise," said Mrs. Peters. "But it won't hurt you to eat it."

"My mom is bringing a great big cake," said Sonny proudly. "I knew about the weenie roast already."

"I did too," said Kevin. "My mom is making a Jell-O salad."

"Can we play games at the weenie roast?" asked Tim.

"There is a game we are all going to play," said Mrs. Peters mysteriously. "You will find out about it on Saturday."

The Scouts ate cookies and drank milk in Mrs. Peters's kitchen. They tried to guess what the game was. But all Mrs. Peters said was "Wait and see."

Everyone wanted to talk to the twins, but Rachel and Tracy wouldn't let anyone else near them.

"Bossy," said Lisa.

At the end of the meeting the Scouts all joined hands. They sang the Pee Wee

Scout song and said the Pee Wee Scout pledge.

Rachel grabbed Kenny's hand and Tracy grabbed Patty's.

Rat's knees! thought Molly. She wanted to know the twins too. Rachel and Tracy always had to be first at everything.

CHAPTER 3

One-legged Race

"**D**o twins really like the same food?" Lisa asked Patty on the way home.

"My cousin knows twins and they can both sing real good," said Tim to Kenny.

"My aunt knows some twins and nobody can tell them apart, not even their own mother," boasted Roger. "Once the wrong one got penicillin pills."

Molly was glad that Rachel and Tracy

got a ride home so the other Pee Wees could walk with Patty and Kenny.

"I don't know any twins," she confided to Patty.

"Now you do," said Patty shyly.

That made Molly feel good all over. This new girl was nice. Molly hoped she would be her friend.

"We're not identical," said Kenny. "Twins that like the same food and stuff are identical."

The Pee Wees had to think about that. Twin talk was brand-new to all of them. No twins had ever been in Troop 23 before.

"You'll like Pee Wees," said Molly. "And Saturday is our big Pee Wee weenie roast."

On Saturday Molly ran to the window as soon as she woke up. The sun was shining. The sky was bright blue.

September could be a funny month, her mother said. It could be sunny, or it could even snow.

Some of the maple leaves were just changing color and the sun made them bright red. The air felt chilly, and Molly got goose bumps when she opened her window.

I can wear my new sweater to the weenie roast, she thought.

The Pee Wees couldn't think of anything else all morning except the picnic. What game were they going to play? Would there be prizes? The Pee Wees' phones were ringing off the hook. They called each other up.

All of them wanted to leave earlier than eleven o'clock.

*   *   *

At last the car was loaded and Molly's dad started for Jefferson Park. Molly bounced up and down in the backseat.

Rachel got to the park at the same time Molly did. Her father drove her in a big blue Cadillac.

Rat's knees! thought Molly. Rachel will probably have a new sweater for the picnic too.

"Look," said Rachel, getting out of her car and standing like a model in the parking lot. "These are designer sweat pants. They are for runners."

Molly looked at the stripes on the sweat pants. She looked at the matching top.

A hex on Rachel! She always had to have something better than anyone else.

The Pee Wees' bright red scarves looked pretty in the sun. Molly felt good wearing one of them.

The twins had matching jeans.

Lisa had overalls.

Sonny had on a matching knit outfit
that looked funny for a boy, Molly thought.
The other boys were already laughing at
him. The mothers were frowning at the
laughing boys.

"Don't tease Sonny," Kevin's mother said.

He's a mama's boy, Molly thought. Easy to tease.

Molly tried to see if Mrs. Peters had a maternity outfit on. She couldn't tell. It was just a loose blouse.

The dads were busy lighting the charcoal grills.

Mrs. Peters was passing out gunnysacks for the one-legged race. "First we'll race," she said. "Then everyone will have a good appetite."

Mr. Peters was there too. "This will be fun," he said.

"Yuck," said Rachel. "I don't want to put my legs into that dirty gunnysack. I'll ruin my pants."

Molly chuckled to herself. Now Rachel's designer pants would be all covered up with a sack during the race.

"Line up on this line!" shouted Mr. Peters.

All the Pee Wees lined up in their sacks. Lucky lined up too.

"Lucky needs a sack," called Roger. "Four legs aren't fair."

Fair or not, Lucky did not want a sack over his legs. "Yip! Yip!" He barked his high puppy bark.

"Get ready . . . get set . . ." called Mrs. Peters. "GO!"

The Pee Wees jumped like kangaroos.

They hopped like rabbits.

They even rolled.

Lisa's sack came off and tripped her.

Molly's sack scratched her skin. It felt awful.

Some grain was still in Tracy's sack, and it made her sneeze. Her nose ran so much, she had to quit the race.

The rest of the Pee Wees neared the finish line.

Molly was in the lead.

Patty was coming up second.

Kenny and Mary Beth jumped close behind.

Molly pretended she was tired and

slowed down. She wanted Patty to win so that she would like the Pee Wees. But when Molly slowed down, Patty kept hopping. Right into Molly!

Smack! Bang! Crash!

Down they went! Patty fell on top of Molly. Then Mary Beth and Kenny moved up.

Someone else went over the finish line.

It was Mary Beth!

Molly had let Mary Beth win instead of Patty.

"Rat's knees!" shouted Molly, getting to her feet. "That's the last time I let someone else win.

"It should have been me!"

CHAPTER 4

Football Fever

The mothers came running over to see if Molly and Patty were okay. Mrs. Peters brushed them off.

"What happened?" she asked.

"Did you trip over something?"

"I tripped over Molly," said Patty, giggling.

Molly didn't say anything. She could have won the race by herself. Rats!

Everyone ran over to Mary Beth and congratulated her. They all shook her hand. She was Molly's friend. It was okay that she won by accident.

But Molly wanted to scream, It was really me! I was the real winner!

"Why did you stop before you got to the finish line?" demanded Rachel. "I saw you. You just stopped, plunk. At the end."

"I got tired," said Molly.

Rachel was too nosy. And too smart. Molly thought no one saw her let someone else win.

"That was sure dumb," said Rachel. "Like you wanted to let someone else win."

A hex on Rachel.

Molly frowned.

Hex, hex, hex.

Tim collected the sacks. Parents bustled

around putting paper plates on the picnic tables. Something on the grill smelled good.

"Yum," said Rachel, rubbing her stomach.

"Now," said Mrs. Peters. "I will show you how to make Indian corn."

She pointed to a basket of fresh corn.

It was still in the husk.

On the cob.

"I know how to husk corn," said Kevin.

"Indians did not husk their corn," said Mrs. Peters. "We will just tie the ends together with a wire, and put it right into the fire to roast."

"It will burn," said Rachel.

"You'll see," said Mrs. Peters wisely.

She showed the Scouts how to tie the ends of the leaves together. Then she let them each put their own cob onto the gray coals.

"We just let it roast now," she said.

"We'll be Indian Scouts," said Roger, doing a war dance. Kevin beat on an imaginary tom-tom.

The other Scouts joined him. "Boom, boom, boom."

Soon they would be eating real Indian food. Molly wondered what it was like to be an Indian girl long ago.

While the corn roasted, Mrs. Peters told them about the Indians. She read them a story about a brave Indian boy named White Fish. The parents listened too.

Then she closed the book and said, "Now for the big news."

The Pee Wees gathered around Mrs. Peters.

This must be the surprise, thought Molly. It must be about the game they were going to play.

"The big news," said Mrs. Peters, "is that soon we are going to play football against another Pee Wee Scout troop. We are going to play Troop 15 from Oakdale."

Oakdale was a suburb.

"My cousin lives in Oakdale," said Tim.

"It will be Pee Wee football," said Mrs. Peters. "No one will tackle anyone. No one will get hurt. We will take turns kicking the ball and trying to get it over the goal line."

Roger cheered loudly. "Yeah! We'll win!" he said.

"We will need lots of practice in order to win," said Kevin's father.

"When is the game?" asked Kenny.

"Can people come and watch?" shouted Tracy.

"Can I be the cheerleader?" shouted Rachel.

Rat's knees! thought Molly. Of course Rachel wanted to be the cheerleader! She liked lots of attention.

"The game is in two weeks," said Mrs. Peters. "And we will need a cheerleader.

"We will sell tickets for one dollar each so that the Pee Wees can help the children's hospital. Last month we earned money to help the pet shelter. This time I thought it would be nice to help a hospital. That is part of being a Pee Wee Scout. To help others who need us."

"Yeah!" shouted Lisa's uncle.

Everyone cheered.

"That will be fun, and helpful at the same time," said Mrs. Baker, the twins' mother.

What a surprise, thought Molly. Not only a game, but a game with real tickets. A game with another Pee Wee Scout troop.

The Pee Wees would be football stars.

One troop or the other!

CHAPTER 5

Cheese Louise

"Time to eat!" called Mrs. Peters. She handed each Scout two small weenies to roast on the end of a stick.

"These are baby weenies," scoffed Roger.

"They are Pee Wee weenies," said Mrs. Betz, who was helping to serve the food.

Molly held her weenies over the gray coals until they got fat and juicy. Then

33

she popped them into the little buns
Sonny's mother had passed out.

"Where are the french fries?" cried Sonny. "We can't eat hot dogs without french fries."

"No one has french fries at a weenie roast," said Molly.

Sonny pouted.

What a baby, Molly thought.

"We don't have a deep fryer here in the park," his mother explained patiently.

The other Pee Wees giggled.

"French fries come from restaurants," said Roger.

"I've had french fries at picnics," boasted Rachel.

"We have Indian corn instead," said Mr. Peters. "It is much better for you." He took the corn out of the fire with big tongs. He heaped it on a big platter.

Mr. Peters showed the Scouts how to take the corn out of the husk.

It was golden and juicy.

The Pee Wees put butter and salt on the corn.

"Yum!" said Molly.

"French fries would be better," muttered Rachel. "With ketchup."

While they were eating, they talked about the big game.

"We have to practice as much as we can after school," said Mrs. Peters. "On the playground, or in the park. We don't want Troop 15 to beat us."

"But someone has to lose," said Mrs. Betz. "The important thing is team spirit. We have to try as hard as we can. Then we will feel good even if we lose."

"I won't feel good if we lose," whispered Molly to Mary Beth.

"It's more fun to win," said Mary Beth.

That reminded Molly of the one-legged race, and she felt mad all over again.

"Mr. Peters will be the coach," said

Mrs. Peters. "Every day when he comes home from work he will help coach the players."

Some of the other dads said they would help too.

"At our next meeting we will choose cheerleaders and make banners and write some cheers," said Mrs. Peters. "We may even make pom-poms."

"Oh, dear!" shouted Mrs. Betz. "I forgot the cheese for the weenies."

She jumped to her feet and got out a squeeze tube of cheese. She ran from one Scout to another, squeezing cheese on the weenies that were not eaten.

"Yuck!" said Rachel, hiding her weenie under her sweater. "That looks gross. It's probably full of preservatives. My dad won't let me eat preservatives."

Squeeze, squeeze, squeeze, splotch!

Out came the yellow cheese in ribbons on top of the weenies.

"It's protein," Mrs. Betz explained. "It adds vitamins and minerals to your food."

The Pee Wees made faces. Molly wished she could steal the cheese squeezer. It would be fun to decorate things. Maybe even Rachel's nose!

Now Mrs. Betz was squirting cheese on the parents' weenies.

"Whoops! That's enough, Louise," said Mrs. Peters.

Louise! Sonny's mother's name was Louise! Louise with the cheese! thought Molly. Cheese Louise!

Molly whispered it to Mary Beth, and they began to giggle.

Mary Beth whispered Cheese Louise to Rachel, and Rachel said, "I'm telling." But she didn't.

Soon all the Pee Wees were running around singing "Cheese Louise," and "Squeeze that cheese, Louise," and even "Cheezy Louisey."

They rolled on the grass and down a nearby hill, they were giggling so hard.

All but Sonny. Poor Sonny, thought Molly.

After dinner the Scouts helped clean up the park. They picked up paper plates and litter and ends of buns. They threw them all away. They packed up the things to go home and put them into cars.

After they had roasted marshmallows, the fathers put out the fires, and they all settled down to practice football.

Mr. Peters showed everyone how to kick the ball high and far. They used a soccer ball.

"Over the goal line!" shouted Mr. Peters.

Everyone took a turn.

Sonny kicked the ball backward over his head.

Molly kicked the ball far, but not far enough.

Kenny kicked it sideways out of the park, and Mr. Peters shouted "Foul!"

Rachel missed the ball altogether. "I don't like sports," she said.

"Ha, that's just because you missed the ball," said Tracy. "Sour grapes."

The best player seemed to be Roger. He was the biggest and the strongest.

"All of you will get better, the more you practice," said Mr. Peters.

The Pee Wees were tired. They could hardly stand up in a circle to say the Pee Wee Scout pledge and sing the Pee Wee Scout song.

Molly wanted to get home and fall into bed. She needed all the sleep she could

get. So she could be strong enough to kick a touchdown in the big game!

CHAPTER 6

Team Spirit

Every day after school the Pee Wees dashed to the park. They practiced before Mr. Peters came and more after he came.

Roger even practiced football in the morning before school. He worked hard.

One morning he fell asleep during math.

"It is good to win," said Mrs. Harris, "but it isn't good to miss math."

After that, Roger's mother said he couldn't practice before school. "You need your sleep," she said.

"I've got too much homework to do before I can practice," grumbled Molly to Mary Beth. "Second grade is hard work. It isn't easy stuff like first grade. Anyway, Roger will win for our team," she said.

But at the next Pee Wee Scout meeting, Mrs. Peters said they could not win without the whole team working together.

"One person can't do it," she said. "Team spirit is what we need. First thing today we will have a pep rally," she said.

The Scouts followed Mrs. Peters out into the yard. She passed out sheets of paper with cheers on them.

The Pee Wees could not read all of the words. But Mrs. Peters read them through

over and over again until they could say
the cheers by heart.

"Go team go! Go team go!
Troop 23 will lead the show."

"Louder!" Mrs. Peters said.
Troop 23 shouted louder and louder.
The next cheer was:

"Roger, Roger, he's our man.
If he can't do it, Kevin can!
Kevin, Kevin, he's our man.
If he can't do it, Tracy can!
Tracy, Tracy, she's our man.
If she can't do it, Rachel can!"

The Pee Wees shouted the chant until
they had called out the names of all the
Scouts in Troop 23. Their voices were
hoarse.

Rachel waved her hand wildly. "Mrs. Peters, we need a cheerleader!"

"Who can twirl a baton?" asked Mrs. Peters.

Rachel waved her hand again. No one else could twirl a baton.

"I can tap dance too," she said proudly.

"We don't need a tap dancer on the field, Rachel. But you can lead the cheers if you have a baton and if you can get a red dress."

Red was Troop 23's Scout color. All their kerchiefs were red.

"I have a red dress," said Rachel. "I wore it in my recital."

"Fine," said Mrs. Peters. "The next time we practice at the field, you bring your dress and baton.

"Now, we can use some pom-pom people too," said Mrs. Peters. "Even though you'll all be playing in the game, it would be nice to have a show at halftime."

All the Scouts waved their hands again. Mrs. Peters chose Tim and Tracy and Kenny.

Rats, thought Molly. She wanted to be a pom-pom person. She couldn't twirl a baton or lead the cheers or wave pom-poms. And she didn't have time to practice kicking the ball.

46

There was nothing left for Molly to do.

Mrs. Peters noticed how sad she looked and said, "It is up to the rest of you to have team spirit!"

But how could she have team spirit if she wasn't part of the game? Molly wondered.

Yet, as the meeting went on she couldn't help getting excited about the big game. They would make banners and pom-poms.

Soon everyone was in high spirits.

"I know one of the kids in Troop 15," said Roger. "He told me that they started practicing for the game way last week."

Mrs. Peters looked worried. "That means we have to try twice as hard," she said. "It won't be easy to beat those Pee Wees."

Mrs. Peters passed out paper and scissors and glue to make banners. She showed the Pee Wees how to cut strips of crepe paper, wind them around their hands, and tie them. Then she showed them how to cut them to make red pom-poms.

It took practice to do them right.

Molly's first pom-pom turned out flat. It looked like a flat, round pancake!

Molly looked at Rachel's. Hers was big and bouncy. It did not look like a pancake. It looked like a pom-pom.

Rachel made another one.

Kevin used too much paper, Molly noticed. He always had big ideas. Bigger-the-better ideas.

But his pom-pom was too thick. It looked like a beach ball.

"That's no pom-pom," shouted Roger. "That's a life raft!"

All the Pee Wees giggled.

When they had finished, Mrs. Peters and Mrs. Betz chose the best pom-poms. And the best banners.

Molly's banner was chosen! Her team spirit came back.

Sonny's pom-poms were the best. Mrs. Betz chose them.

"He's so artistic," she said.

The Scouts said their Pee Wee Scout pledge and sang their Pee Wee Scout song.

Then they trooped to the field together to meet Mr. Peters for practice.

The best pom-poms in the world wouldn't help if Troop 23 did not play well. They had to practice hard to beat the Oakdale Pee Wees.

CHAPTER **7**

An Indian Summer Day

The next morning on the way to school, Tracy caught up with Molly. "We have to get moving if we are going to win next week," she said. "Let's get permission to practice at lunchtime."

Tracy was bossy. Molly hated to be ordered around. She wanted to eat her lunch, not practice football.

"There's no time," said Molly.

Tracy stamped her foot on the sidewalk. "Where is your team spirit?" she demanded. "My dad works with one of the Troop 15 dads, and he said they make about ten touchdowns every day when they practice."

Molly frowned. That sounded bad.

Tracy went on. "My dad said they have some big kids on their team. With long legs. They can kick the ball over the goal line right from the starting line."

"No one could kick that far," said Molly. "Nobody's legs are that long."

"They are too. Do you think my dad made that up?"

Tracy ran ahead to catch up with Lisa and Rachel and Tim. She probably wants to scare them with her dad's stories too, thought Molly.

At the bus stop, Molly saw Kevin waiting to cross the street.

"Hey!" he yelled. "How many tickets did you sell?"

A new worry, Molly thought. She hated to admit she had only sold tickets to her own mom and dad.

Two dollars.

That would not help the children's hospital much. All it would buy would be some Kleenex, maybe. Or a couple of aspirin.

"I've got this big campaign," said Kevin. "I sell them to my uncle and the guy next door, and then they sell them at work. That way I don't have to do all the work."

Leave it to Kevin to think of some scheme, thought Molly. Some plan that would earn money while Kevin was playing. He'll probably be a businessman when he grows up.

It was not a bad idea, though.

Molly could ask her aunt who worked

in an office to sell them, and her dad could take some to work.

Her grandma would take a ticket, but she might not come to the game because she had a bad leg.

Molly counted up tickets in her head.

After school she went door-to-door on a block where no Pee Wee Scouts lived. Then she ran to football practice. By the time she got home to do her homework it was getting dark.

"Cheese Louise!" she said out loud in her room. "There's a lot of work to do when you are in second grade."

She began to miss all the free time she'd had when she was little. Back then, no one expected anything of her. Just play, play, play. All day long.

At the next Scout meeting Rachel wore her red dress. It sparkled and dazzled like a diamond necklace. Rachel kept twirling around in it.

Mrs. Peters showed the Pee Wees the badges for Team Spirit.

Molly knew she had to sell more tickets! She was full of team spirit by now.

Then Mrs. Peters showed the Scouts the badge for Best Player. Everyone knew who would get that.

"Roger," said Sonny. "He's the best player."

"He practices the most," added Mrs. Peters.

"He's the biggest," Kenny pointed out.

The football game drew closer and closer. Every day Molly checked off the days on her calendar. Every day the Scouts sold more tickets.

"I sold fifteen," said Tim. "All on our block."

"I sold twenty-one," said Patty.

Molly wondered how a new girl could sell so many tickets. The Bakers didn't even know people on their block yet.

"The Welcome Wagon helped," Kenny explained.

"I can't wait to see these other Pee Wees," said Roger to Molly after school the next day. "I wonder if they're really good."

"Maybe they're babies," said Molly. "Real little kids. Maybe they are all first graders."

But then Molly remembered Tracy's words. They were big.

"I heard they are good," said Sonny.

Molly wanted to say "shut up" to Sonny, but she didn't. No one wanted to hear they were good.

*   *   *

At last the day of the game came.

What if it is raining? thought Molly when she woke up. She was afraid to open her eyes. But when she did, bright sunshine streamed in through her window.

Her mom came in. She had clean jeans and a new shirt for Molly. Her red Pee Wee kerchief had been ironed neatly.

"It's a perfect day!" said Mrs. Duff. "It is warm and sunny out, with a blue, blue sky. This is a real Indian summer day."

Molly thought of the weenie roast and the Indian corn and the Indian stories Mrs. Peters had told.

Now it was Indian summer! Molly felt good all over. They would win.

Troop 23 had to win!

CHAPTER **8**

The Blue Pee Wees

Troop 23 jumped out of cars and ran into the park. Their red scarves flashed in the summer sunlight. People sat on folding chairs and canvas stools. They stood all around the edge of the field. Some wore hats and blew whistles. Some wore football jerseys. Others waved banners with troop numbers on them.

Tiny and Lucky came along too!

59

One big dog and one little dog.

The Troop 23 mascots wore red bows around their necks.

This is different from practice, thought Molly. There were strangers at the game. Some people came to cheer for Troop 15. They didn't want Troop 23 to win.

"Look!" shouted Roger. "Those other Pee Wees have uniforms!"

As the other team got off a big yellow bus, everyone stared. They looked like a real team, like the Minnesota Vikings.

They had blue striped football uniforms on. Around their necks were their Pee Wee scarves. But they were blue instead of red.

Even Mr. Peters looked surprised. "Uniforms won't help them win," he said. "It is team spirit that wins a game."

But Troop 23 wasn't so sure. Those Pee

Wees in blue looked big. They looked old. Plus, they had uniforms.

"They look tough," said Tracy. She sniffed. Maybe she was allergic to the new Pee Wees!

Molly's stomach felt nervous. Like when she had to take a test in school. Or go to the dentist to have a cavity filled. Even if it didn't hurt, her stomach didn't know that.

A group of moms and dads were on the field in a circle. They were waving flags and chanting:

"Troop 15, Troop 15!
They play fair and they play clean."

"Well, so do we," said Rachel, sticking out her tongue.

Mrs. Peters was getting her own cheer-leaders ready. The pom-pom Pee Wees looked scared. But Rachel marched right out onto the field and began twirling her baton. The sunlight caught her dress and made it sparkle.

Sparkle, sparkle, sparkle.

No one could miss Rachel.

She had on little white boots. With tassels. On her head was a shiny crown. On her wrist she wore her gold bracelet.

Everything flashed and sparkled when she twirled.

"Go, team!" Rachel shouted, lifting her knees.

Then she did three cartwheels in a row!

She looked like a pinwheel turning round and round, her arms and legs spinning.

Troop 23 was proud.

"Rachel is really talented," said Mary Beth.

"It's good that we have a cheerleader,"

said Mrs. Peters. "Troop 15 doesn't have one."

Then Rachel started throwing kisses!

What a ham, thought Molly.

"What a ham," said Kevin.

"Hey!" said Molly. She looked at Kevin in surprise.

"Yeeeaaah team!" called Rachel as she walked off the field with her hair bouncing in the September sun.

"Arf!" barked Tiny.

"Yip! Yip!" barked Lucky.

"Now," said Mr. Peters. "Let's go over the rules one last time."

The Scouts tried to listen, but there was too much to watch.

"The main thing to remember is not to touch the ball except to kick it," said Mr. Peters.

"And don't touch anyone else. There's no tackling in Pee Wee football. Just kick the football over their goal line. If you tackle anyone, or pick up the ball, you will have a penalty called. If you get ten penalties, you will be out of the game."

More and more people came as Mr. Peters talked.

Mrs. Peters was counting the Pee Wees. "Someone is missing," she said.

The Scouts looked around.

"Sonny!" shouted Molly.

She was right. Sonny was nowhere in sight.

"Maybe he got scared," said Roger. "He's scared of dogs, he might be scared of football too."

Just when Mrs. Peters was about to go find a phone, someone came running down the road.

The Scouts stared.

The person came nearer and nearer.

"That is no one we know," said Lisa.

The person had something on his body. Something big. Something gray or white.

"It's a ghost," said Mary Beth softly.

"It's bright daylight out," scoffed Rachel. "Ghosts don't hang around in daylight."

"It's a burglar!" cried Kenny. "He has a mask over his face, and it isn't Halloween yet."

"Oh, no! Why is it coming here?" shouted Patty.

It was true. The burglar-ghost was running toward them as fast as he could with the big thing on.

He was shouting something. The words sounded like "My mom had to go to work. I had to come by myself."

Did burglars have moms that worked? That voice sounded familiar to Molly. She thought and thought. Then she knew. They all knew!

It was Sonny!

CHAPTER 9

Sonny Scores

"**W**hat in the world . . ." said Mrs. Peters, looking puzzled.

Sonny was not a ghost or a burglar. He just looked like one.

He wore huge football shoulder pads. They stood out on his body like giant wings.

His large white shirt had a number 23 on it. Under it he wore a huge chest protector.

On his head was a helmet with a plastic face guard. It looked more like a cage than a mask!

"My mom had to go to work," Sonny repeated, all out of breath. "I had to come alone."

The Pee Wees could not take their eyes off Sonny. Suddenly they all burst into laughter, he looked so funny.

"My mom said football is dangerous. She made me wear this big suit because they didn't have my size."

Mrs. Peters put her arm around Sonny. He looked like he might cry.

"Pee Wee football is not dangerous," she said. "I think you can take that off."

Sonny shook his head. "I promised," he said. "My mom would kill me if I didn't wear it."

"You've got wings!" shouted Roger, pointing.

"We have to pull together," said Mr. Peters.

Molly thought he would say, No matter what Sonny is wearing.

The Scouts heard a loud, sharp whistle blow from the field. It was the other coach.

It was time for the game to start!

"Line up!" shouted Mr. Peters.

Rachel had her jeans on now, Molly noticed. Even a cheerleader had to play ball.

The two teams lined up facing each other.

Red and blue.

Mr. Peters threw the round ball into the air. BUMP! It came down on Sonny's head.

Then it hit the ground, and a big boy from Troop 15 with a 6 on his back kicked it hard.

The ball flew through the air. It landed halfway to the goal line!

71

Team 23 ran as fast as they could to try to kick the ball the other way. But number 6 got there first.

He gave it one big kick and it sailed over the goal line like a breeze.

"One to nothing!" shouted their coach, shaking number 6's hand.

"Darn!" said Molly. "We are off to a bad start."

The whistle blew. The Pee Wees lined up again. Poof! The ball came down again.

"Kick it!" screamed Rachel to Molly.

The ball was at Molly's feet. She kicked. But she didn't kick the ball. Something was in the way.

It was Sonny.

Sonny and his big suit.

Molly tripped over him and tumbled to the ground.

"A penalty on Molly," called Mr. Peters.

Molly felt like crying. It wasn't her fault that big dumb Sonny got in the way.

But she couldn't cry. Ballplayers didn't cry. Not when they had team spirit.

Instead, she ran after the ball.

"Pow!" yelled Roger, giving the ball a good kick. It sailed toward the goal line. The Scouts raced after it. The ball slowed down right before the goal line. Molly gave it a little kick.

It went over.

Touchdown!

"One to one!" shouted Mr. Peters.

The team clapped and cheered for Molly. The dogs barked. The people watching blew whistles and waved flags.

Her parents shouted:

"Molly! Molly! She's all right!"

Molly felt wonderful! She did not feel like crying now. She felt like a football hero!

It was fun to play the other Scout troop. It was easy too.

"That was good," said Mary Beth when the coaches called time out.

"Roger was the one who kicked it really far," said Molly.

"But you kicked it over the line," said Rachel.

Rat's knees! It felt good to hear nice words from Rachel.

The Pee Wees drank some Kool-Aid and then lined up again.

Out flew the ball. Whooosh!

It stopped in front of Sonny. He gave it a huge kick. The ball sailed through the air, farther than it had ever gone. It went right over the goal line!

But no one cheered.

"Dummy!" yelled Roger. "You kicked it over the wrong goal line!"

The blue Pee Wees laughed and cheered. "Touchdown!" they shouted.

"Two to one," said the other coach with a chuckle. "For us!"

"I got turned around," Sonny admitted.

"Hey, Wings," called a girl from the other team. "You're an angel to make a touchdown for us!"

"Time out," called Mr. Peters.

He did not look happy.

CHAPTER 10

Break That Tie!

Molly thought Mr. Peters would yell at Sonny for being so dumb. But he didn't. He put his arm around Sonny's padded shoulders and told him to keep his eye on his team's line.

The Pee Wees played on. Troop 15 kicked another touchdown. Then Troop 23 got one.

Kevin was called out of the game because

he got ten penalties. He was a good player, but too rough. The other team clapped. They wanted the best red players out.

Pretty soon the blue Pee Wees got ahead by three points.

"We're losing!" cried Tracy. "We'll never catch up."

But then the big blue Pee Wee, number 6, grabbed Kenny's arm and tried to get the ball. It was his tenth penalty. He was out of the game.

"Now that he's gone," said Roger, "we can win."

Roger knows a lot about football, thought Molly.

He will be the hero.

Sure enough, Roger kicked two touchdowns in a row. The Pee Wees cheered. The parents cheered too.

Then Molly kicked the ball over the line again. She tied the game.

It was five to five!

Time was running out.

"Whoever gets a touchdown now will win the game for us!" called Mr. Peters. Then he called time out.

Rachel got into her sparkly outfit. The pom-pom Pee Wees followed her out onto the field.

They sang:

"Kenny! Kenny! He's our man.
If he can't do it, Molly can.
Molly, Molly, she's our man.
If she can't do it, Roger can.
Roger, Roger, he's our man.
If he can't do it, NOBODY can!
Yeah, Roger!"

Everyone was bursting with team spirit now! They dashed back to the field to break the tie.

The ball bounced onto the field. Troop 15 kicked it. Then Sonny kicked it the right way. Then Tracy kicked it farther.

But the other team sent it back the other way. Would it go over?

No!

Molly ran up and gave it a hard kick. POW! But the ball hit Roger and bounced to the ground. Roger kicked, but he missed it.

The crowd groaned. "Break that tie, break that tie," chanted the spectators.

All of a sudden Patty raced up to the ball and kicked it as hard as she could. Molly heard a loud SMACK! The ball sailed over the goal line, breaking the tie!

The crowd roared! The dogs barked, running in circles.

Patty was the hero! She broke the tie!

Little Patty Baker! She hadn't even kicked the ball once until then.

Mr. Peters ran onto the field and picked up Patty. He put her on his shoulders. Everyone yelled and screamed.

They chanted:

"Patty! Patty! She's our man.
If she can't do it, NOBODY can!"

The ball game was over. Troop 23 had won.

Mrs. Peters ran around throwing red confetti up in the air.

Roger yelled:

"Patty cake, Patty cake, Baker's man,
She wins a game like none of us can!"

Molly felt good all over. She had tried to let the new girl win, and it didn't work. But then she tried to win herself, and the new girl won!

The blue Pee Wees did not seem to feel bad that they had lost. They all came running up to shake Patty's hand and to congratulate Troop 23.

They don't seem so big and tough now, thought Molly. They seem just like us. Like regular Pee Wees!

Mrs. Peters held up her hand for quiet. "I think now is a good time to give out the badge for the winning player. You all played very well, but it was Patty who broke that tie and won the game for us."

Patty turned pink.

She's shy, thought Molly.

Mrs. Peters pinned the badge on Patty's scarf.

Everybody clapped. Even Troop 15.

"Good work, Patty cake," said Roger.

"Now you all get badges for team spirit," said Mrs. Peters.

The other troop leader passed out badges for team spirit too.

"The important thing isn't to win," said Mr. Peters. "But to have a good time and pull together.

"We had a good time, and we helped the sick children at the hospital."

All the Pee Wees clapped.

"But it was fun to cream those Pee Wees, wasn't it?" whispered Roger to Molly.

Molly nodded. Pulling together is good, but winning is better!

The two troops of Pee Wee Scouts joined together in a giant circle on the field under the blue, blue sky.

They alternated. One red Pee Wee, one blue Pee Wee.

One red, one blue, all around the circle.

"We look beautiful!" shouted Molly.

Everyone laughed.

They did look beautiful.

Even Sonny with his wings.

All together they said the Pee Wee Scout pledge.

Then they sang the Pee Wee Scout song.

Their voices rang out clearly in the autumn air. It sounded twice as good with two troops of Pee Wees!

The big day was over.

It was time to go home.

"I'm hungry," said Sonny. "For a big plate of french fries!"

"I think we all deserve french fries!" said Mr. Peters. "Let's go to Fun-and-Fries and I'll treat everybody to all the french fries they can eat!"

"Yeah!" yelled the Pee Wees.

"Arf! Arf!" barked Tiny.

Lucky went, "Yip! Yip!"

The dogs were hungry too.

Pee Wee Scout Song

♪ ♪ ♪ (to the tune of ♪ ♪ ♪
"Old MacDonald Had a Farm")

Scouts are helpers, Scouts have fun,
Pee Wee, Pee Wee Scouts!
We sing and play when work is done,
Pee Wee, Pee Wee Scouts!

With a good deed here,
And an errand there,
Here a hand, there a hand,
Everywhere a good hand.

Scouts are helpers, Scouts have fun,
Pee Wee, Pee Wee Scouts!

Pee Wee Scout Pledge

We love our country
And our home,
Our school and neighbors too.

As Pee Wee Scouts
We pledge our best
In everything we do.